THE
WOLFMAN AND
THE CLOWN

HELEN GANLY

ANDRE DEUTSCH

In memory of my father
Geoffrey Robinson
and for my artist friends in Czechoslovakia

First published in 1990 by
André Deutsch Limited
105–106 Great Russell Street London WC1B 3LJ

Typeset by AKM Associates (UK) Ltd
Ajmal House, Hayes Road, Southall, London

Printed in Hong Kong

One day Mrs Ray was in her front garden when she noticed a noisy group of children outside a nearby house. As she watched, one of the children ran up to the window, peeped in and ran back to the others.

Mrs Ray was curious. She asked the children what
they were doing. They all began talking at once.
"Please, miss, we've seen them. They're in there. In
that house."
"Who are?" asked Mrs Ray.
"The wolfman and the clown," Peter said. "I saw the
wolfman first. He went into the house and looked out
of the window. I told my friend James."

"I went to look," said James "but the curtains were shut so I banged on the door. The wolfman peered through the curtains. He looked very frightening! He had lots of grey hair and glaring eyes and big teeth!"

"My name's Gwen," said another girl. "I looked through the window to see the clown. He was dancing round and round with the wolfman so fast they made me feel dizzy and I ran back to the others."

"I'm Ali," said a boy. "At first I couldn't see anything because it was so dark, but then I saw the wolfman open a cupboard and evil looking green smoke came out and the clown was walking about on his hands with yellow lights flashing out of his shoes."

"My name's Rosamund," said another girl quietly. "I was frightened when I looked. "The wolfman was waving his arms about and the clown was crouched on the floor. There were horrible faces staring from the walls. I ran away!"

"I was the last one," said a boy called Tai Wan. "I didn't want to go, but everyone said it was my turn. There were shadows of strange monsters flickering on the walls, and weird wailings and moanings. The wolfman and the clown were whirling round in the middle of the room. I ran back as fast as I could."

Mrs Ray was puzzled. She didn't know what to think. Just then a police car turned into the road. "Look Miss," said Melanie, "let's tell the police – they'll know what to do!" The children were so sure that Mrs Ray agreed. "All right," she said. "I'll stop the police. You decide who will tell them what you've seen."

The car stopped. "What's going on?" asked the driver. "It's that house," said Mrs Ray. "There's something . . ." Melanie told the policewoman what had happened. "It's the wolfman and the clown," she said. "They're in there. We all saw them, dancing and making smoke and . . ."

The policewoman looked at the children. "There's no wolfman or clown in there," she said firmly. "The only person in that house is old Mr Kelly. You've probably frightened *him* – peering through the windows and banging on his door. I know what gave you the idea, though. You've seen the advertisement in the High Street, haven't you? It's for a film, and it's got a picture of a wolfman and a clown on it and says 'Reward offered if you see these two'."

The children looked silently at each other. "So that's it,"
said Mrs Ray. "I think we'd better go and apologise."
They went up to Mr Kelly's door. The paint was faded and
the knocker tarnished – as though no one ever used it.

They had to knock several times before the door was opened by an old man, with shaggy grey hair and a beard. He looked frightened, but Mrs Ray explained what had happened. He smiled. "There's no wolfman or clown here," he said. "Only me and my cat. Perhaps you'd like to come in and see for yourselves."

It was dark in the room, but the children could see the
sun shining on the garden wall and the houses
opposite through the shabby lace curtains.

As their eyes became used to the gloom they could see that the room was full of interesting things. Theatre posters and photographs of actors and actresses were pinned up all over the walls.

Cloaks and strange costumes hung from hangers. Peter noticed a typewriter and papers on a chest of drawers – what did Mr Kelly do for a living?

There were masks and hats piled high on a chest of drawers. Coloured cloths and cushions were flung down on the chairs and sofas.

Over in the corner of the room stood a big wooden box.
Mr Kelly lifted up the lid.

"Look at this!" said Melanie excitedly, as Mr Kelly
removed the top cloth.

It was filled with even more interesting things – wigs and hats, a suit of armour, boots and shoes, guns and swords, and a basket full of rings, brooches, and necklaces.

"I am not a wolfman or a clown," said Mr Kelly.
"but I can be lots of other people." He pulled a wig, a
beard, a purple cloak, a sword and a crown out of the
box and there, before the children, stood an old King.

Mr Kelly took a costume from one of the hangers. "Would one of you like to try this?" he asked. Ali stepped forward. It was a bit big, but he looked very fine all the same. The others pushed forward, eager to try on masks, wigs and robes.

At last it was time to go. "Perhaps Mrs Ray will bring you again," said Mr Kelly. "I have lots more treasures to show you." The children said goodbye, turning to wave and promising they would come again.

Mrs Ray followed them thoughtfully. She had glanced up the stairs as she left and thought she'd glimpsed – had she? – a pair of flashing shoes and silk pantaloons fade into the gloom.